The Two Uncles of Pablo

The Two Uncles
of Pablo

HARRY BEHN

ILLUSTRATED BY MEL SILVERMAN

HARCOURT, BRACE AND COMPANY, NEW YORK

© *1959 by Harry Behn*

First edition

Library of Congress Catalog Card Number: 59-8949
Printed in the United States of America by The Murray Printing Company

FOR ALICE

Contents

Pablo at Home

At siesta time, every creature goes to its own bit of shade to rest from the hot bright sun. When doves wake up again and call to other doves, when a dusty hen shakes her feathers and steps out from her own place under the nopal cactus, then Pablo crawls out from under his pepper tree, his black hair dusty and spotted with dry pink pepper berries. He walks over to the house and takes a drink from the *olla* that hangs full of cool water under the *portal*.

Each morning Maria, plump and pretty as a dove, fills the olla at the spring and carries it on her head back to the house. Now she sits under the portal, her wide skirt spread out, softly singing as she grinds corn on a stone *metate*. Maria is Pablo's mother.

Pablo's baby sister, Josefina, lies there on the soft cool dust, kicking her fat little legs.

His father, Felipe, has gone out to the cornfield where he is cutting down the dry stalks.

Now Pablo's bare feet take him along the path to the cornfield. He helps his father tie a bundle of stalks together with a piece of vine. He holds a loop of the vine across his forehead, and his father helps him lift the bundle up on his back. He has to bend far over to carry it, but he is proud that he can. His father carries a much bigger load.

When all the dry stalks are cut and carried up beside the house, Pablo and Felipe break off the ripe ears of corn. Then they scrape the dry kernels into the storage bin.

Soon the bin is full to the top, and they cover it with a wooden lid. But there is still more corn. When the last grain is scraped from the last ear, there is a pile of corn on the ground as high as Pablo, who sits there pouring the smooth yellow grains through his fingers.

Now it is evening. Smoke from the fire smells good. Maria is cooking *tortillas* and beans. Over the mountain, a cloud turns gold in the sun. Soon the sun touches only the top leaves of the pepper tree and the flat top leaves of the nopal cactus. The dusty hen calls that she has laid an egg, and Pablo goes out to find it.

After they have eaten their supper, Josefina is only a small sleeping bundle wrapped in her mother's shawl. Maria is happy. She is thinking about the new baby she will have soon.

Felipe is thinking how wonderful it is to have so much corn. Never before has there been enough to last until the next crop. Often they have had only a few beans to eat, and the purple fruit of the nopal cactus. Now there is so much corn that some of it can be sold in the town.

Felipe is thinking about why there is so much corn. He is thinking about a carved stone that stands among the rocks above the spring. This stone has an old name that is never spoken. The summer before, when it was so dry, Felipe gave this stone a present of two ripe figs. Now it has returned to him all this corn. He has not said anything to Maria about why there is so much corn. He knows she would not like what he did.

12

Felipe's Plan

"I have saved the best seed for planting," said Felipe, "but there is still more than our bin will hold. I think there will be two sacks to sell in the town."

"We could make a bigger storage place," Maria suggested softly.

Felipe went out into the moonlight. He went out to look once more at the corn piled up like a little mountain. He wanted to sell enough corn to buy a rooster. The sound of a hen clucking to her chicks would be pleasant in the evening. It would be pleasant, too, to hear a rooster crowing in the early morning. But there must be something to feed them all, so Felipe decided to sell only one sack of corn.

Pablo came out into the moonlight, and Felipe said, "Tomorrow I will go to the town and sell one sack of corn."

Pablo had never been to the town. He hoped his father would take him this time. But Felipe had not been to the town very often himself, and the adventure scared even him a little. "You must stay here with your mother," he said.

He was thinking about the long way up to the road, through *maguey* plants on the hillside, and the longer way along the road to the town. If he started tonight, he thought, he would see, far away in the sunrise, the pointed tower of the church and the low houses against the hill among the trees. As he walked into the market place, the early bells would be ringing. "I think I will leave now," he said, "and walk through the moonlight."

Pablo helped his father pour handfuls of corn into a sack. When the sack was loosely filled, Felipe tied a string around the open end and shifted the corn so that there was some in both ends to make it easier to carry over his shoulder.

All this time, Felipe was thinking how tired his bare feet would be, walking so far, and he said, "If I bought a few chicks, that would not take all the corn. Perhaps one of them would grow up to be a rooster. If I bought only chicks, perhaps I could also buy a piece of leather to make into sandals. That is what I will do. I will leave now while the ground is cool and come home tomorrow wearing sandals."

Suddenly Felipe felt very tired and decided not to leave until morning. "Perhaps," he said, "who knows, someday we will have a burro."

When Pablo and his father were asleep on their straw mats, with only their noses showing outside their *serapes*, Maria looked at them with great love. She did not want Felipe to go to the town. When she was a little girl, she had lived there. She remembered all the bad things that happened to people. It was true, almost everyone had sandals to wear, and there were fiestas. But sometimes when the men drank *pulque*, they became too brave and picked up burning fireworks. She used to like the fire-

14

works—the castles of sparks and the whistling snakes of fire that went spinning up into the night—until one time her father picked up a spinning piece of fire, and it burned him, and he died.

While Pablo and Felipe were sleeping, Maria lit a candle and placed it before a small figure that stood in a niche in the wall of the portal. The niche was painted blue, like a shell of summer sky, and a beautiful lady stood in it, dreaming of all the wonderful things there are in heaven. To this sweet kind lady, Maria said, "I do not want my Felipe to go to the town." Then she lay down and slept, smiling because she knew that in the morning he would decide not to go to the town after all.

Morning light spread over the mountain in wide rays like the feathers of a golden bird. On top of one flat leaf of cactus, a canyon wren was singing its sweet song.

When Pablo came out of the house, doves flew up from the pile of corn where they had been feasting. On the ground sat the dusty hen, reaching her neck out, pecking grains of corn, one at a time, gulping them down. She could hardly swallow. When she tried to stand up, she sat down again and looked ashamed of herself. Where her wishbone used to stick out, now she had a fat little sack full of corn, and she wasn't feeling very well.

But Pablo knew what to do. He picked up a handful of stones as small as grains of corn. He opened the hen's beak and poured them down inside her pink throat. He knew that chickens have no teeth, so they need stones inside them to chew up their food.

Pablo put the hen in the shade. Then he and his father

16

scooped all the loose corn into another sack until it was tight full. Together they lifted it up on top of the storage bin.

Felipe looked at the loosely filled sack of corn he had decided to sell and said, "You must take good care of your mother while I am gone."

Now the sun was pouring its warm light down the hillside. Felipe looked out in the direction he would soon be going. He had decided now to buy a rooster old enough to crow. But he was thinking how hot it would be, walking all day under the sun. He was thinking how wonderful it would be if he had a burro to ride. "If we had two burros," he said to Pablo, "I would take you with me." The sun was already burning down very hot, so Felipe decided to wait until evening before he went to the town.

Pablo looked into the sunshine. He was thinking about what his father had said. Someday they would both have burros, and they would ride together to the town.

While he was looking into the sunshine, Pablo saw something he could hardly believe. Far away, trotting along in a shining cloud of pink dust down the hillside, came a burro!

The Visitor

Felipe and Maria and Pablo stood outside their fence of cactus, waiting, watching, as a man rode down the hillside, his long, flapping legs almost touching the ground as his small burro trotted along.

"I think," said Maria, "that Uncle Silván is coming to visit us."

And that is who it was, Maria's uncle, Silván Ruiz. He sat as far back on the burro as anyone could without falling off. His big mouth was smiling wide in the middle of a few white whiskers. His small eyes twinkled at Maria and Felipe and Pablo, and also at a fig tree that grew beside the house. On this tree there were several green figs and one that was ripe and black and ready to eat.

"Good morning, Maria," said Uncle Silván pleasantly. "Good morning, Felipe." Then he smiled at Pablo. "And this young man, I suppose, is Pablo. Good morning, Pablo."

The boy was so busy looking at the burro that he did not hear Uncle Silván speak to him.

But Uncle Silván's feelings were not hurt. He went right on smiling and said, "Would you mind handing me that ripe fig, Pablito, if you please, before it falls to the earth and goes to waste?"

18

Pablo did not pick the fig, but Felipe did. He gave it to Uncle Silván, who popped it into his mouth. Chewing the fig and dribbling a little on his whiskers, he put down his legs and stepped off the burro. He shook hands with Felipe and then with Maria.

Pablo was still looking at the burro, who stood patiently on his small gray hoofs, not looking at anything.

"What is your name?" Pablo asked the burro, as if the animal could answer him.

Uncle Silván laughed at the boy who seemed to think an animal could speak like a person. But he stopped laughing when the burro, who had not been looking at anything, turned his head and looked at Pablo and wiggled his soft gray muzzle as if he were trying to answer such a polite and natural question.

Uncle Silván was surprised. He said, "That burro is called Angelito, and as long as I have been acquainted with him, this is the first time I have ever seen him look at a person. Usually he is too busy thinking."

Pablo patted Angelito's soft woolly neck and said, "You must be very thirsty. Come with me and I will show you the way to the spring." The boy walked away down the path through the cactus. With small, careful steps, Angelito followed him.

Uncle Silván scratched his whiskers and shook his head. "A boy like that, who can speak to animals, might go a long way in the world. But first, someone would have to teach him politeness. Pablo must also learn to speak to persons when they speak to him."

Felipe and Maria felt ashamed. Politely they asked Uncle Silván to come in and sit down under their portal. He came in and sat down and took off his sandals and rubbed the mud off his big feet, while Maria cooked him some tortillas.

When Uncle Silván had eaten everything in sight to eat and had picked his teeth for a while, he said to Maria and Felipe, "I suppose you are wondering why I have come all this long way out here to visit you."

It was true; Maria had been wondering. She felt that something bad must have happened or was about to happen.

"Well," said Uncle Silván, taking a dirty rumpled envelope from under his shirt, "here is a letter for you, Maria. What it says inside no one knows, because my friend Lopez, who drives a bus and can read, would not open it and read it to me. He said that anyone who opened it except Maria Ruiz would be sent to prison. That is why I have brought it out here for you to open."

The Letter

Maria had never had a letter before. She was afraid of it. But Uncle Silván put the envelope in her hands and made her fingers tear it open. Then he took out the paper and unfolded it and stared at the marks of writing, wondering what they meant. "If we could read this letter," he said, "who knows—it might tell us that some rich Ruiz has died and left his *hacienda* and all his cattle to Maria, perhaps even a herd of a hundred fighting bulls!"

"Who knows," said Felipe.

Suddenly Uncle Silván stood up and shouted angrily at Felipe, waving his big hands. "I suppose you want me to go all the way into the town and have Lopez read this letter to me and then come all the way back here to tell you what it says!"

"No," said Felipe, "I don't expect you to do that. I was going to the town anyway. I will go with you. Your friend can tell me what the letter says, and I will come back home and tell Maria what he tells me."

But Maria did not want Felipe to go to the town. She took the letter from Uncle Silván and put it inside the front of her dress. "I don't care what is in the letter," she said. "Good or bad, it is not important."

Uncle Silván's mouth opened wide and closed before he shouted, "Important! Do you tell me a great herd of beautiful black fighting bulls standing in grass up to their horns is not important?"

By this time, Pablo had come back from the spring. He was riding Angelito, who had taken a drink and was now thoughtfully chewing a mouthful of weeds. The boy had heard everything Uncle Silván had said and listened now to what he was still saying. "If you had any intelligence," the old man was shouting at Maria and Felipe, "you would know how to read! In the town, let me tell you, every child can read! But you, you are a disgrace to the family of Ruiz! You make me ashamed." He turned away from all of them and made a sound of great sorrow.

Felipe and Maria looked at the ground.

Pablo slid off the burro and sat down beside them.

"Is it hard to learn how to read?" he asked Uncle Silván.

"Hard? Not at all. In the town, every child can read. I have heard them myself, many times."

"Then why can't *you*?"

Uncle Silván opened his mouth a few times before he asked, "Am I a child?"

"Why didn't you learn when you were?"

"Because"—the old man waved his hands—"I had more important things to do."

"What?" asked Pablo.

Uncle Silván stood up and shouted at Maria, "Give Felipe the letter!"

"No," she said.

Without looking at her, Felipe spoke softly. "The burro could carry my sack of corn. Perhaps Uncle Silván would let me ride part of the way."

"Felipe can ride *all* the way!" said Uncle Silván. "Now give me the letter, and we will go!"

"No," said Maria.

Uncle Silván sat down again. He sat down like someone dropping a sack of corn. "Then I will stay here until you become more reasonable. I will stay here all the rest of my life, if necessary. Pay no attention to me. I need only a few crumbs to eat. I have my serape. I will sleep here on the portal. Sleep? No. I will never sleep again until I know what is in that letter." He was very sad.

Felipe and Maria still looked at the ground. They did not say anything. But Pablo did. To Uncle Silván he said, "My mother wants my father to stay at home until our new baby comes. But *I* do not have to be here for a baby to be born."

Uncle Silván held his hands out in surprise to find everything settled so simply. "Give Pablo the letter," he said to Maria.

Again she said no. But this time, Uncle Silván did not seem to mind. He scratched his whiskers and smiled. He was thinking how useful a strong boy like Pablo could be to him in San Miguel. There were many jobs a boy could do there — jobs a dignified person like himself could not do, such as cutting alfalfa to feed the burros on market day, or shining rich people's shoes in the town gardens. "You are an intelligent boy, Pablo," he said. "You must come to San Miguel with me and stay there and go to

24

school. You can take your mother's letter with you. When you have learned to read, you can come back home and read it to her. Yes?"

"No," said Maria.

Uncle Silván was disgusted. "It is a sad thing," he grumbled, "when a boy's own mother wants him to remain a disgrace to her family. Felipe, now, is different. He has a sack of corn to sell. But what is he going to do with that sack of corn? He is going to let Pablo sell it to pay for his pencil and his book when he goes to school. Even I, poor old Uncle Silván, do you know what I am going to do for this boy because he wants to amount to something? Do you know what I intend to give him? I intend to give him a burro of his own!" He waved to Angelito and said, "There is your burro, Pablo, to ride into the town and back home again as often as you want to."

Pablo could hardly believe what he heard. He went over to Angelito and put his arms gently around the little animal's neck.

"Now," said Uncle Silván to Maria, "give Pablo the letter!"

"When Pablo has learned to read," said Maria quietly, "when he comes home again, I will give him the letter, and he can read it to us."

Uncle Silván took in a deep breath. At last he said pleasantly, "Very well." He called to Felipe, "Bring the sack of corn."

Felipe brought the loosely filled sack of corn and heaved it across Angelito's back.

Pablo stood looking at his mother, at the geranium

flower growing in a tin can, at the dusty hen who still sat in the shade, at everything he loved. The hen reached her neck out and pecked at an ant. It crawled away. She was too full to care. A dove called in the pepper tree.

Pablo went into the house and came out with his folded serape. He kissed his mother's hand, and his father's hand. He put his serape across Angelito's back and stood there patting him and looking into the sun.

Uncle Silván scratched his whiskers and smiled. He shook Felipe's hand and Maria's hand and said, "Someday you will see, the family of Ruiz will be proud of Pablo."

Then they were gone, into the morning sun. Pablo was riding Angelito, sitting as far back as he could without falling off. Behind him, Uncle Silván was walking along in a shining cloud of pink dust.

"A good thing has happened, I think," said Felipe.

"Who knows," said Maria.

On the Road

Up through the maguey plants, Pablo rode silently. The only sounds were the sleepy whirring of grasshoppers and the stepping along of Angelito's small hoofs and the scuffing of Uncle Silván's sandals. No one said anything. Pablo did not even look at anything except Angelito's gently bobbing ears. Soon they came to the road.

All morning, the road curved on through cornfields crossed with hedges of cactus and maguey. Sometimes they went down into steep *barrancas* full of *mesquite* trees and wild flowers, and then up again. Once they left the road and had a drink of water from a pool among some rocks. Another time, they saw a cloud of dust far ahead and moved off the road and waited until a bus went by. It was the first time Pablo had ever seen a bus. To him it seemed like a big house blown along by a noisy wind. He did not let Uncle Silván see how it frightened him.

When they climbed back on the road, Pablo wanted Uncle Silván to ride. But Uncle Silván did not want to ride. He seemed to enjoy walking along in a cloud of dust, so Pablo climbed back up on Angelito and rode.

Sometimes Uncle Silván moaned. One time, he sat down and rubbed his feet. Another time, he took off one of his sandals that flapped and tried to fix it. He didn't seem to know how. But Pablo did. He bit off a short piece of string from the sack of corn and tied it around the broken leather of the sandal. Still the tired old man would not ride. "No," he said, "I gave you that burro. He is not mine to ride any more. I'll hobble along somehow."

Pablo felt ashamed. And he knew that Uncle Silván, for some reason, wanted him to feel ashamed.

After the sun had gone down, they rested. Uncle Silván sat with his back against a rock. Pablo poked a piece of branch up into a tall cactus plant, and some of its fruit fell to the ground. With a flake of rock, he peeled the fruit and they ate it, even Angelito.

Uncle Silván sighed. "When your mother lives in a big hacienda, I only hope she remembers who brought her that letter and who gave her little boy such a fine burro."

Now Pablo knew why the tired old man was having such a pleasant time, walking behind in the dust. It would be something to tell people, in case Maria did not invite him to live in her hacienda.

Pablo did not believe the letter said anything about a hacienda. It was foolish to expect something for no more reason than just wanting it to be true. Uncle Silván was really a very foolish old man.

Of course, Pablo expected to go to school. But that was not foolish. Someday he would read the letter. It would probably not be for his mother at all. Then Uncle Silván would be angry and sorry that he had given Angelito away. He would tell everyone how he had walked all day

on a broken sandal, while a big strong boy like Pablo rode.

Pablo knew what Uncle Silván was thinking. But he was not angry. He was only sorry for anyone so foolish.

When the stars came out, they started on again and went a long way, silently, toward the town.

Suddenly Pablo woke up. He had been riding along sound asleep. Uncle Silván was standing beside him, looking down into a cup of darkness, where a few lights shone no brighter than the stars. "That is the town. That is San Miguel," said the tired old man. He and Pablo wrapped themselves in their serapes and lay down on the ground and slept. Angelito went quietly to sleep, too, standing with his head and his ears drooping.

Dreams

Sometime in the night, Pablo heard roosters crowing and bells ringing, and he dreamed they were reciting lessons together, bells and roosters, lessons so old that only books remembered them.

When he woke up, a new sun was shining on his face. Uncle Silván was sitting on a wall on the edge of the hill. When Angelito saw that Pablo was awake, he stopped chewing and wiggled his soft gray muzzle as if he were saying, "Good morning, Pablo."

"Good morning, Angelito." The boy smiled. "Thank you for carrying me all that long way." He rubbed the sleep out of his eyes and looked about him. Everything was like a dream. On all sides there were fields of sunflowers, and far away against the sky was a wall of mountains shining in the sun. Between the mountains and the sunflowers, in a valley full of trees, houses crowded down through shadow to a pointed tower, a tower that rose high above everything, its pink stone shining in the sun.

Pablo folded his serape and put it under a flat stone. If he could not find a place to sleep in the town, he would come back up here and be quite happy among the sunflowers.

He started to say good morning to Uncle Silván, but the old man was remembering when he was a boy, when he first smelled this same dusty smell of sunflowers, when he first heard these same crickets chirping. He loved the sounds that floated up through the bright morning. But most of all, he loved the far away happy voices of children on their way to school.

When Uncle Silván was Pablo's age, he had been sure that someday he would be rich and own a big hacienda. He had been sure that when he walked in the town gardens on Sunday mornings, everyone would bow to him and call him Don Silván.

But that is not how it turned out. He had always been too busy dreaming about his big hacienda, or singing sad songs with *mariachi* singers. He had never seemed to find time to go to school. He had never learned how to read— or to do anything very well except to sing in *cantinas*. That is why he had no land in his old age, or even a small house of his own.

He had many Ruiz relatives, and he stayed with them sometimes, for a few days. When he left them after a visit, they would count their spoons because sometimes he put such things in his pocket. Then for quite a while, he would not feel welcome in that house. This morning he could not think of a single house where he and Pablo would be welcome.

Most nights he slept in a hut that nobody owned. There was only part of a roof and hardly any flat floor among the piles of corn husks and fallen plaster. He did have a straw mat to sleep on. He kept it tucked up under a rafter. If he left it down, which he did sometimes, pigs wandered in and slept on it. It was quite a comfortable place. But he did not think Pablo would like it. So he did what Pablo had done. He folded his serape and put it under a flat stone among the sunflowers.

At the moment, Uncle Silván had less than almost anybody else in the world. But he still dreamed that someday he would live in a beautiful hacienda and wear a *sombrero* with spangles.

Adios, Angelito!

Pablo understood animals. He understood Uncle Silván, too, and knew what he was thinking. He went over and quietly sat down beside the old man and said, "Thank you for giving me Angelito."

Uncle Silván sighed. "It was nothing. You must believe I was thinking only of your happiness, no matter what happens." He looked nervously up the road.

Angelito was turning both his ears toward the top of the hill.

The little burro lifted his head, opened his mouth, and curled his lips back from his big teeth. Then he took in a long breath and brayed with a tremendous roar. "Haw! Hee-haw!" shouted Angelito over and over until, with a grunt, he ran out of breath.

Over the edge of the hill came a brown burro, and another, and another. Three brown burros came over the hill with loads of wood on their backs, and behind them a dark-faced young man wearing a brown serape and a straw sombrero. The young man looked strangely at Uncle Silván. He spoke to his burros, and they stopped. Uncle Silván was more nervous than ever.

Suddenly the young man shouted, "You are a thief, Silván Ruiz! You said you would return Angelito to me in one hour, and you have been gone with him for two nights and two days! I have lost many loads of wood because of you. It will do you no good to promise me half or even all of some big rancho that does not exist. This time I am going to have you put in jail!" The young man was very excited.

"Chucho, forgive me!" begged Uncle Silván. "I must have lost track of time. One hour, two days, ten years, all seem the same to a tired old man who has nothing left to live for."

Chucho noticed the sack hung loosely across Angelito's back. "I see you have something there. Is it corn?"

"Yes," said the old man with a sigh, "it is corn."

Chucho picked a sunflower and pulled it apart while he thought. "All right," he said. "If you give me that corn, I will not have you put in jail."

Uncle Silván groaned. "It is not my corn."

"It is mine," said Pablo.

Chucho looked at the boy.

"You may have the corn," said Pablo.

"Would you give me that corn simply to keep this dirty old man from going to jail?"

"Yes," said Pablo.

Chucho spoke to his four burros, three brown ones with wood and one gray one with a sack of corn. They went down the road toward the town, and he followed them.

With small careful steps, not looking at Pablo, or at anything, Angelito walked away down the road.

"*Adios,* Angelito," said Pablo.

The Town

It was bad enough when a burro you thought was your
friend didn't care about you. But it was worse to see an
old man sitting there in the daylight, crying.

"If you would only believe me," Uncle Silván said,
wiping his nose on his sleeve. "When I gave Angelito to
you, I completely forgot that he belonged to Chucho. I
was thinking only of some way to make you happy,
Pablito. You believe your poor old Uncle Silván, don't
you?"

"No," said Pablo honestly.

The old man brushed the tears out of his eyes and said,
"You'll see. You'll see what I am going to do for you."

"What?" asked the boy.

Uncle Silván opened his mouth wide while he tried to
think what he was going to do.

"What are you going to do?" asked Pablo.

Uncle Silván scratched his whiskers. Then he said. "You
want to go to school, don't you? All right, I am going to
arrange it. I am going to take you to the teacher and tell
her what is in your mother's letter! Do you know what
that letter says, Pablo? It says that someday a big Ruiz
hacienda is going to be yours!" He laughed happily.
"When that teacher knows how rich you are going to be,

39

she will give you your book and pencil and teach you how to read! Someday it will mean nothing to you to pay everything back to her, and more!"

Pablo looked sadly at Uncle Silván and walked away down the hill.

The old man was surprised at Pablo's bad manners. It was not polite to walk away when an older person was speaking. With his sandal flapping, he trotted along behind the boy. "You don't understand," he said. "You have very important relatives. One of them will surely die someday and leave you something. Is it a lie to tell the teacher so?"

"Yes, it is," said Pablo, and he kept on walking down the hill.

Uncle Silván flapped along a little way behind. He kept saying over and over, "I am only thinking of you, Pablo!" Down beside a stream of water they went, across a bridge, past a stone tank where women were chattering like birds as they washed clothes. Down a steep, rough, cobbled street went Pablo and Uncle Silván, between the walls of houses built in rows. Some of the walls were plastered and painted pink and blue and dark red, and some showed the pieces of rock and brick they were built of, like the spots on spotted animals.

In every doorway, babies sprawled happily in the coolness. Beyond these shady doorways, there was always a sunlit patio full of green leaves and flowers. All the trees that showed from the top of the hill seemed to be growing in these green patios.

40

Pablo noticed that no children his own age were to be seen anywhere. He knew why. They were all in school. But everywhere, grown people were walking on the narrow sidewalks or in the street. Many of them, especially the old ones, were barefoot. Those who wore shoes or sandals walked carefully because in some places pieces of the sidewalks weren't there at all.

Almost everyone was building or mending something, or carrying something—a baked yam wrapped in a piece of newspaper or a green leaf, or a heavy sack of cement, or a tall cane pole with candied crab-apples stuck on it like red flowers. Other people had other things to sell— peanuts, or tin sieves, or serapes, or brooms, or ollas—and all of them called out in voices like a song how good their wares were. They had grown or gathered or made everything themselves, so they knew how good they were.

With so much excitement on every side, Pablo almost forgot about Uncle Silván still flapping along behind him, not even trying to explain to him any more.

Pablo had even almost forgotten about Angelito. Once he felt sad, when he passed a train of burros loaded high with cut grass, and another time when he had to walk around two burros waiting patiently on the sidewalk outside a cantina. Out of this doorway came a damp, unpleasant smell. It was a place where rough men drank pulque and sang sad songs.

When Uncle Silván passed this cantina, he stopped. He turned back, pushed the swinging doors open a little, and peeked inside. There were no mariachi singers there,

so he let the doors swing shut again and went flapping along after Pablo, trying to walk a little taller and more dignified.

At last Pablo came to a garden in the middle of a square. In the center of this garden, carpenters were nailing down a new floor on the bandstand, while several men were blowing music out of dented brass horns of all shapes and sizes. They never played their tune very long at a time. They had to move about to keep out of the way of the carpenters.

In this garden there were many trees with big dark shiny leaves, and tall monkey trees full of chirping birds with long tails. Under the trees, people walked slowly or sat in the shade. Some of them were eating *paletas,* colored ice on sticks.

Beyond this plaza, Pablo saw the tower that he had

seen from the top of the hill. Its points of pink stone were carved into shapes like flowers. It went up and up against the blue sky. In its arches there were bells of all sizes. The biggest bell was taller than the man who stood up there, waiting to ring it. A small bell began to ring, and the man beside the big bell swung it, and its deep slow tone boomed out, and soon all the bells were ringing, high and low, slow and fast, their voices tumbling over each other. While the bells rang, the long-tailed birds flew up out of the trees and circled in the sky.

At last the bells stopped banging, and the birds glided down again to the trees. As the humming of the bells faded away, the only sounds were the chirping of the birds and the pounding of hammers and the whirring of an automobile as it went by. Then Pablo noticed that Uncle Silván was sitting on the bench beside him.

The old man was very unhappy. "I don't blame you for being ashamed of me," he said. "I did lie to you. I knew all the time that Angelito was not mine. Forgive me, Pablo, and I will promise you something. I will promise to buy Angelito for you. I will buy him from Chucho and give him to you. Then you can ride him back home and tell Felipe and Maria that Uncle Silván is not so bad after all. Yes?"

"When will you do this?" asked Pablo.

Uncle Silván scratched his whiskers, trying to think how long it would take. Suddenly he smiled and said, "When you have learned how to read!"

Pablo had no idea how long this would take. And he didn't really believe Uncle Silván would ever buy Angelito for him. But he did know the old man was trying to be kind, so he said, "Thank you."

"Do you forgive me?" asked Uncle Silván.

"Of course," said Pablo.

With a happy smile bursting out of his whiskers, the old man stood up and said, "Now I must find some kind of work to do to earn the money to buy Angelito for you."

With his sandal flapping, Uncle Silván walked away, straight and dignified, up the street toward the cantina.

Miss Iris

Sitting alone in the plaza, Pablo felt very lonely. He began to remember how happy he had been, working with his father, not saying very much, but feeling good about the earth. He remembered how his mother smiled. He remembered Josefina's little face like a flower, and he wondered when he would ever see them all again.

A man walked by under the trees, singing out that he had paletas to sell, and Pablo forgot that he was lonely. He thought that if only he could taste one paleta, a red one, he would never be lonely again. He was very hungry.

Out in the country, he would know where to find plants and seeds to eat. But in the town, every crumb had to be bought. And he didn't have even one *cinco,* that small coin worth less than a penny.

The market was full of shops selling every kind of food. On the street, women sat beside charcoal fires, cooking sizzling *tacos* and other delicious things. Under the arcades, men sold pecans cracked half open, or cakes, or bread, or colored candy made from cactus or coconut or figs or orchid bulbs. But Pablo did not have even one cinco. By now he was so hungry, he thought he could eat rocks the way his dusty hen did, and he began to look around to see what sort of work he might do to earn some money.

He didn't have to look very far. A large, friendly woman with eyes as blue as morning-glories, and a basket full of bananas and pineapples and bottles of milk and vegetables, asked him to carry her basket for her. She spoke a strange language. But Pablo understood. He took the heavy basket and put it on his shoulder and walked beside her. They smiled at each other, and she spoke to him in Spanish. "What is your name?" she asked. And he told her, "Pablo Pico Ruiz."

"Pico is your father's name?"

"Yes. And Ruiz is my mother's."

"Do you live in San Miguel?"

"No. My home is out by the mountain."

"Has your family come in town to buy things?"

He tried not to sound afraid or lonely. "No," he said.

"Are you in town alone, Pablo?" she asked, and he nodded.

"Why?"

He decided not to tell her about Uncle Silván, or Angelito, or the letter that had come to his mother. But he did tell her the most important reason. "I want to learn how to read."

The woman was also one who understood. She reminded him of Angelito, the way she looked at nothing when she said, "I don't suppose you have eaten this morning."

He did not think it would be polite to say, so they both walked along, just thinking, like Angelito.

She opened a gate, and they walked across her patio. She went into her kitchen, and he followed her and put the basket on the table. She asked him to sit down and told her maid to fix him some food. Then she went on inside her house.

The food that Pablo was soon eating was very good. He ate slowly, so the maid would not see how hungry he was. When he stopped eating, he was as full as his dusty hen had been the morning before.

The woman came back into the kitchen and smiled. "I want you to take this to a friend of mine," she said, and handed him a letter. "I want you to help him if you can. If you do, he may help you. If he doesn't, I will." She gave him a large copper coin. "This is your pay for bringing home my basket."

"Thank you," he said.

Then she told him where to take the letter to her friend, Señor Pico, who was called Don Francisco.

It wasn't far. Past the gate to the bull-fighting ring and beyond the corner, there was the high wall that went all around the place of Don Francisco Pico. It was one of the old spotted walls showing the stone it was made of. In some places, cactus and wild flowers grew on top of it.

Pablo walked beside the wall, wondering if Señor Pico might be some relative of his father. He did not think so. There were many people named Pico, almost as many as there were named Ruiz.

Pablo stopped. There was something strange about this wall. In one place, there had once been a door. Now it was filled up with old bricks and rocks, or almost filled. At the top, there was still a small hole about as big as a boy's face. Pablo did what every other child in the town had done at some time. He climbed up the jagged rocks and bricks and looked through the hole.

What he saw, beyond a garden, was a long low house with deep shady *portales,* where vines blazed with red and orange and purple blossoms. Everywhere there were flowers, and over the flowers, butterflies floated and danced in the sun, small white ones, quick brown ones, and large lazy black ones with yellow stripes. In a grove of old trees covered with moss, birds flew singing, and far back among ferns, fountains made a cool, moist, shadowy music.

Pablo had never seen anything so beautiful.

Don Francisco

Not only was the garden like a dream, the old man with hair as white as a cloud, who sat there only a little way inside the wall, seemed just as strange. It must be Don Francisco! He sat very straight on a low stool, holding a book on his knees, and he was writing in the book. He had a narrow face with a nose like a bird's beak. His eyes were large and dark, and he was very sad. That is what Pablo felt about Don Francisco, that he was the saddest person he had ever seen.

"Why are you so sad?" asked the boy.

Don Francisco was not surprised to be spoken to. He was not angry or pleased. He seemed used to having part of a small boy's face peer at him through this hole in his wall.

"Who is it this time?" he asked.

"Pablo," said the boy.

"I don't believe we have met before, have we, Pablo?"

"No, señor."

The white-haired old gentleman sighed and began to write again in his book. He was so old that the skin on his face seemed to be worn very thin.

"The lady who asked me to bring you this letter told me I might be able to help you," said Pablo.

Don Francisco closed his book and put it aside and went over to the wall. "Let me see the letter," he said, and Pablo gave it to him through the hole.

When he had read the letter, Don Francisco went back and sat down again on his stool. He looked up at the part of the boy's face that he could see, and said, "Miss Iris thinks you could help me, Pablo Pico. How do you think you could help me?"

"I don't know, señor. The only work I have ever done is to help my father grow things."

"As you see, my garden is well cared for."

"It is very beautiful. But I could plant you some chilis and melons. Yes?"

Don Francisco did not say anything. He began to write again in his book. Pablo did not move, and the old gentleman said quietly, "If you will excuse me now, I must go back to my work. Good-by, Pablo."

Pablo slid down to the street. He sat against the wall. He wondered how anyone could be so sad when he lived in a garden that was so beautiful.

What the boy did not know was that Don Francisco Pico was a poet, and very rich, and famous all over the world.

Miss Iris, who had been so kind to Pablo, knew Don Francisco very well. She liked the sad poems he wrote. But she liked the cheerful ones that sometimes slipped out of the end of his pen even better. She wanted him to write more of them. She thought that children would like them. But Don Francisco said he didn't care whether children liked them or not, he did not like children. Miss Iris thought that he would like children better if he would bother to know more about them than just their small faces peeking at him through the hole in his wall. That is why she had sent Pablo with a letter to him.

But Don Francisco was too busy writing a sad poem to be interested even in a friendly little boy whose name was Pablo Pico.

The Two Uncles

Somewhere down the hill, a bell rang and a burst of happy shouting drifted up through the sunshine, and Pablo forgot about Don Francisco. He thought how wonderful it would be to play games with other children. He wondered what kind of game made them sound like birds hopping about and chirping in a treetop. While Pablo was wondering about this, Uncle Silván came along the street, eating a bunch of grapes.

The old man sat down beside the boy and listened to the happy sounds drifting up from the school. Now and then, he popped a grape into his mouth and chewed it, dribbling a little on his whiskers. He ate the last grape and threw the stem away. Then he glanced at Pablo and felt ashamed for eating all the grapes himself. "Are you hungry?" he asked.

Pablo smiled. "No. I carried a basket for a lady, and she gave me lots of food—and this piece of money." He showed Uncle Silván the coin Miss Iris had given him.

Uncle Silván smiled. He took the fifty-*centavo* piece and said, "This gives us a good start toward buying Angelito. Such a fine burro may cost us a hundred *pesos*. But I think between us we can manage it." He put the coin in his pocket.

"You told me *you* were going to buy Angelito," said Pablo.

Uncle Silván looked disappointed. "Between us, we could buy him much sooner."

The bell rang again, and the voices of the children became silent. Soon they were inside the school, singing about a dove. It was a peaceful song. Outside, real doves were cooing in the leafy shade.

"I think," said the boy, "that I would like to use my own money to pay for my book and pencil and go to school. When I have learned how to read, then you may buy Angelito for me. But I don't expect you to," he added.

The old man said proudly, "Didn't I promise you I would?" He stood up and started to walk away.

Pablo stood up, too. "I would like to keep my own money," he said.

Uncle Silván did not seem to hear Pablo, he was staring so hard at the wall. "Do you know whose wall this is?" he asked in a whisper.

"Yes."

"Whose?"

"Señor Pico's."

"Do you know that he is the uncle of your father?"

"I did not know that," said Pablo.

"Well, he is. And that makes him your great-uncle. Also, he is the richest man in San Miguel, and the meanest." Uncle Silván stared at the hole in the wall as if he expected some horrible lizard to come crawling out of it. Suddenly he grew very excited and shouted, "What has he ever done for you, Pablo? Has he bought you a burro? Has he sent you to school? No! From that stubborn, mean old man you may expect nothing! Why? Because he is a Pico!"

Pablo glanced at the wall, and there were Don Francisco's sad dark eyes peering out through the hole.

"Good morning, Silván," said Don Francisco.

Uncle Silván tried to pretend he hadn't heard these polite words, but in spite of himself he grumbled, "Good morning."

"It has been a long time since I have seen you," said Don Francisco, "although I have heard your voice late at night, singing loud enough to set all the dogs in town to barking."

Uncle Silván grabbed Pablo's arm and said, "Come along, Pablo. That old bird-beak is trying to make me mad. In a moment, he will say something insulting about the Ruiz family."

"I was coming to that," said Don Francisco.

Uncle Silván waved his big hands and shouted, "This boy is a Ruiz!"

"He looks to be every inch a Pico to me."

Uncle Silván hitched tighter the rope that held up his pants. "There's nothing Pico about him! Only an accident makes you the uncle of his father, a disgrace that had best be forgotten. Come along, Pablo."

But Pablo was curious to know why these two old men were so angry at each other. He looked at Don Francisco's eyes peering out through the hole in the wall. Then he looked at Uncle Silván who had kicked off his broken sandal and was sitting on the sidewalk trying to put it back on his foot. "Why don't you like each other?" Pablo asked both of them.

Don Francisco said nothing. But Uncle Silván jumped up and shouted, "Look at him, sitting all day in his garden, scribbling in a book instead of doing honest work like other people! What has he ever done for a boy who can talk to animals, a boy who wants to amount to something? Has he bought you a burro? Has he sent you to school?"

"Have you?" asked Don Francisco.

Uncle Silván's mouth opened wide. Then he shut it. Suddenly he wasn't angry any more. He smiled and said, "Not yet, señor. But let me tell you, poor as I am, what I am going to do for Pablo. I am going to buy him the best burro in San Miguel, and I am going to send him to school. Why? Because I am a Ruiz!" He walked a few stiff steps away. Then he turned and called loudly, "Come along, Pablo!"

But there was still something the boy wanted to know. He knew now that Uncle Silván was mad at Don Francisco for being rich. But he did not know why Don Francisco was mad at Uncle Silván. He looked at the dark eyes peering out through the hole and asked, "Are you mad at Uncle Silván because he is poor?"

Don Francisco almost smiled. "Poor? Is he so poor with your fifty-centavo piece in his pocket?"

With a look of great sorrow, Uncle Silván sat down against the wall, where Don Francisco could not see him. He tossed the coin over to Pablo, who picked it up and said to Don Francisco, "He was only keeping it for me so we could buy Angelito between us."

"Of course," said Don Francisco.

"Why don't you like Uncle Silván?" asked Pablo.

"I will tell you why," said Don Francisco, sticking his face a little farther into the hole. "Because ten years ago, he came to me and said he needed some money to buy a guitar. If he had a guitar, he said, he could get a fine job singing with his mariachi friends on the radio, and he would be rich. As you see, he has no guitar. He has never had a guitar—not because I didn't give him plenty of

58

money to buy one. The money I gave him was not a gift. It was pay for a job I asked him to do for me."

Don Francisco stuck one of his slender hands out through the hole in the wall and waved it gently about. "As you see, there used to be a door in this wall. But some children bored a hole in the door and were always peeking through it and bothering me. So I paid your Uncle Silván to take out the door and fill the hole up with rocks and bricks."

"And so I did," grumbled Uncle Silván, "all but that little hole hardly bigger than a mouse hole."

"Yes, he went right to work like a Ruiz! A man came by with a burro, and he borrowed the burro. He tied a rope to the door, and the burro pulled it out of the wall. He loaded the door on the burro and took it down to the market place and sold it. Then he told all the children in town to bring him rocks and old pieces of brick, and he filled up the hole —almost! The children had not brought him quite enough bricks and rocks. It was evening, and they had to go home to their suppers. And so did your Uncle Silván, I suppose, because I never saw him again, since that day ten years ago, until today."

"Hardly bigger than a mouse hole," muttered Uncle Silván.

"But that isn't the whole story," said Don Francisco. "The next morning, a man came to me to collect the money your Uncle Silván had told him I would pay for renting his burro to pull the door out of the wall. And that afternoon, all the children in town came to me to collect the money your Uncle Silván had told them I would pay for

each rock and piece of old brick they had brought him. I paid everyone, of course, because I am a Pico. But since that day, for ten years, children have been peeking at me through this hole, every day reminding me why I do not like Silván Ruiz!"

Uncle Silván held his head between his hands and groaned. Pablo knew the story was true. But there was one thing he still did not understand, and so he asked Don Francisco. "If that small hole has bothered you for so many years, why didn't you have someone else fill it up?"

Don Francisco looked stubbornly out through the hole. "I had already paid Silván to fill it up. It was his responsibility."

Feeling very tired, Uncle Silván got up on his feet and started to walk away, staying close to the wall.

"Has he gone?" asked Don Francisco.

Uncle Silván stopped to listen.

Pablo shook his head.

"Good," said Don Francisco. "I want him to hear this. I want him to hear what I am going to do. I am going to buy your books for you, Pablo, and give you a fine room in my house to live in while you go to school. I am going to help you with your studies, year after year, until you know everything that I know about this world. How does that sound to you, Pablo?"

Pablo did not know what to say. Don Francisco must know a great deal. But everything he knew only made him sad. Pablo glanced along the wall and saw that Uncle Silván was gone.

"Now," said Don Francisco, "if you will come around to my door, my servants will let you in, and we will wash the Ruiz off you and begin to turn you into a Pico."

The old gentleman was surprised to see the boy walk away down the street, looking for Uncle Silván.

The Hole in the Wall

Pablo found Uncle Silván sitting on the edge of the ditch, soaking his feet in the muddy water, moaning about how unfair Don Francisco was to make such a fuss over a hole in his wall hardly bigger than a mouse hole.

Pablo understood Uncle Silván the way he understood animals. He did not blame his dusty hen for being lazy and eating too much corn when she could find it, or dogs for barking at night when they saw a terrible white tiger in the sky and it was only the moon. He did not expect anything else from them, and that is the way he felt about Uncle Silván.

The foolish old man was not always honest, and sometimes he became excited over nothing. He owned less than almost anybody in the world. But he enjoyed a great many things that nobody owned—the smell of sunflowers, and the sounds of birds singing, and children laughing, and roosters crowing, and bells. He did not know very much. He couldn't do anything very well. But most of the time he was happy. And he tried to be kind.

Don Francisco was different. He owned a beautiful garden and a house. He knew almost everything there was to know. But he was sad and not very kind. The only reason he wanted to do so much for Pablo was to make Uncle Silván, who couldn't do it, feel ashamed.

Uncle Silván did feel ashamed. But he didn't mind. One thing he enjoyed more than anything else was feeling sorry for himself.

When the boy sat down beside him, Uncle Silván was surprised. "What are you doing here?" he asked. "I thought you were going to stay with that rich uncle of yours and go to school forever and learn everything there is to know!"

"Someday I might," said Pablo.

"*Someday!*" Uncle Silván gasped. "He asked you *now!*"

"He only wanted to make you feel ashamed," said the boy.

Uncle Silván jumped up. He was very excited. "Are you such a fool that you walked away from a house like that, where food is served to you on plates and where you will have a chance to learn how to become rich?"

"He wanted to wash the Ruiz off me and make me a Pico," said Pablo.

"Why not?" shouted Uncle Silván. "Why not?"

"I don't want to be ashamed of you," said Pablo, "for not finishing a job he paid you to do."

Uncle Silván guessed what Pablo was going to say, and it made him nervous. He enjoyed a great many things. But one thing he did not care for very much was work. Work really bothered him. "I suppose you want me to fill up that hole in Don Francisco's wall!" he shouted angrily. "That hole hardly bigger than a mouse hole!"

"Yes, I do," said Pablo, "and I will help you."

Uncle Silván started to walk away. Then he stopped. "How do you know he *wants* it filled up? How do you know he doesn't *like* to have children watch him sitting there, scribbling in his book and looking sad? How do you know if we filled up that hole, he wouldn't stop being sad and just be unhappy? Do you want to make your poor old Uncle Francisco unhappy?" asked Uncle Silván.

Pablo did not answer. He began to gather rocks and put them in his pockets, so Uncle Silván picked up a few small rocks and put them in his pockets.

Something had to hold the rocks in the hole. There was lots of mud along the edge of the ditch, so they scooped up blobs of it and carried it in their hands up to the wall.

Uncle Silván peeked through the hole. There was no one in the garden—only the sleepy stillness of siesta time and a few black butterflies with yellow spots fluttering lazily over the flowers.

Pablo handed the rocks and mud to Uncle Silván, and in a few minutes the hole was filled up tight. The old man smiled. "Now let that old bird-beak tell me I haven't done what he paid me to do!"

Suddenly, from the other side of the wall, came a wail of anger.

"I told you," whispered Uncle Silván happily. "He didn't want it filled up!"

A Visit to Miss Iris

Uncle Silván started to shout something over the wall. But Pablo asked him not to and walked away. The old man bounced along on his bare feet. He had lost both his sandals somewhere. He laughed, thinking about Don Francisco's being so angry when the hole in his wall wasn't filled up, and then being angry when it was. Don Francisco was a foolish old man.

Pablo was wondering why Don Francisco didn't want any melons and chilis planted in his garden. His flowers, of course, were all happy and beautiful. Miss Iris's garden was the one that needed something done with it. Perhaps *she* would let him plant some melons and chilis. That is what he was going to ask her. He knew how to make plants grow. Ever since he was very small, he had worked with his father, pulling out weeds and spading and pouring water down to thirsty roots.

Suddenly Pablo felt ashamed. Thinking about working in Miss Iris's garden had made him think about his father's having to work alone, with no one to help him or keep him company. He had been so excited about Angelito, and coming to the town, that he had forgotten about his father.

66

He stopped outside the gate to Miss Iris's patio. He could not ask her now to let him work in her garden. He had decided to go back home and help his father until spring.

Uncle Silván came bouncing up hopefully. "Where are we going, Pablo? Is this the house of the lady who gave you that fifty centavos and a nice breakfast?"

Pablo nodded. "Yes. This morning I noticed that her garden needs some work done to it. I think it will take at least a month of hard work to spade up the soil."

"And I know the boy who can do it!" said Uncle Silván proudly. "May I come in with you?" he asked, smoothing his whiskers and knocking a chunk of mud off his elbow.

"Yes," said Pablo. He opened the gate.

Miss Iris was sprinkling her tired flowers. The water ran off the hard ground and made puddles on the path.

She noticed Pablo standing there and turned off the hose. She smiled and started to ask what Don Francisco had said about her letter, when Uncle Silván stepped forward and shook her wet hand.

"This is my Uncle Silván," said the boy.

Miss Iris turned on the hose again and washed off her hand. Then she asked Pablo, "What did Don Francisco say about my letter?"

Uncle Silván snorted like a horse.

Miss Iris looked at him coldly. Then she turned to Pablo and asked, "What did Don Francisco say?"

"I offered to help him, but he did not want me to plant any melons and chilis in his garden."

Miss Iris was amused. "Did he offer to send you to school?"

"Yes. But I have decided not to go to school for a while."

She glanced at Uncle Silván, and the old man said angrily, "He offered to send Pablo to school and let him live in his house and eat food served on plates! But what did this foolish boy do? He said no!"

Miss Iris looked at the boy. Her blue eyes sparkled. "I am glad Don Francisco offered to help you. That is the important thing. But I am glad, too, Pablo, that you want to stand on your own feet. I am proud of you."

So Uncle Silván was proud of him, too. Proudly he patted Pablo's arm. "This is an intelligent boy. He wants to amount to something. He wants to work in your garden."

Miss Iris said, "It certainly needs something done to it."

Uncle Silván picked up a chunk of dry earth and crumbled it in his hand. "What this garden needs," he said, "is a good spading—at least a month of good hard work."

"All right," said Miss Iris to Pablo. "When do you want to start to work?"

"In the spring," said Pablo.

Miss Iris was surprised.

"When I come back to go to school," he said, "after our corn is planted. Tonight I am going back home to help my father."

"Tonight!" shouted Uncle Silván. He backed away nervously.

To Miss Iris, Pablo said, "I thought Uncle Silván might work for you."

She glanced at the dirty old man who seemed scared half to death. "I said nothing about helping your Uncle Silván."

68

"I know," said Pablo, "but if you let him work in your garden, you would help me, too, because then he would have the money to keep a promise he made to me."

"What did he promise you?"

"To buy me a burro named Angelito."

Again she looked at Uncle Silván, who waved his big hands helplessly.

Miss Iris was amused. To Pablo she said, "All right. I will pay your Uncle Silván a month's wages in advance. He can buy Angelito for you this afternoon, and you can ride home on your own burro. When you come back in the spring, then you will go to school, Pablo, and work in my garden. Yes?" Pablo nodded. It seemed to her such a happy idea that she laughed out loud. She was still laughing when she went inside her house to get the money for Uncle Silván.

The old man pushed his bare toes against the hard ground and groaned.

"It is not right to make promises and not keep them," said Pablo.

Uncle Silván spread his arms out helplessly. "I did promise to buy Angelito for you," he said sadly, "after you had learned how to read."

This was true! Pablo had forgotten this part of the promise. He was ashamed. "I'm sorry," he said. "I was not being fair. I will tell Miss Iris you don't need that money after all."

Quickly Uncle Silván said, "No! I wouldn't say that. It would not be right to disappoint her." He smiled. "I did promise to buy Angelito for you. *When* I do doesn't matter. I will buy him this afternoon, and you can ride home on your own burro, and you won't be ashamed of me any more."

Big Business

Uncle Silván had never had so much money at one time in his whole life. In each of his two big hands he held a crumpled bundle of ten-peso bank notes. "This should buy *two* burros"—he smiled—"and still leave us enough to buy a rooster for Felipe and a ribbon for Maria." He laughed happily. "Won't they be surprised to see us come riding down that hill among the maguey plants, on our own burros, with all those presents! Two burros should cost about eighty pesos. How much does that leave us for a rooster and a ribbon?"

"I think we had better take the money back to Miss Iris," said Pablo.

All the happiness fell away from Uncle Silván's face. "I forgot," he said.

The boy was silent.

And Uncle Silván said, "I won't think any more about buying a burro for myself. I will try to make that garden look pretty if it takes all my life to do it. I will work harder than I have ever worked before until I have earned every centavo of this money! You believe me, don't you, Pablo?"

"I think so," said the boy slowly.

Uncle Silván was happy again. "Now that I have only one burro to buy, there will be more money for presents.

Perhaps a pair of sandals for Felipe and *two* ribbons for Maria."

"You had better save something to buy food for yourself."

"Oh, I will, I will! There may even be enough for a guitar. I have always wanted a guitar of my own."

"I think we had better find out first how much it will take to buy Angelito," said the boy.

Uncle Silván smiled slyly. "You watch how I bargain with Chucho! I won't have to pay more than fifty pesos, you will see!"

Pablo wondered.

Coming toward them along the street was a burro loaded with a tremendous bale of cosmos flowers. The burro turned his head a little to one side and took a bite of the blossoms. He didn't bother to chew them but came walking along with the flowers hanging out of his mouth. The small man who walked behind the burro carried two heavy tin cans full of water, slung from a curved pole across his shoulders. This small, patched-up man was laughing. His hair stuck out in tufts through holes in his sombrero.

Uncle Silván went up to him and said, "Good afternoon. We are looking for Chucho. Have you seen him?"

"Yes, I have," said the small man, tipping his worn-out sombrero, "not two minutes ago. He wanted to trade me that gray burro of his for this old black one of mine and give me twenty pesos to boot. I told him I would sell my grandmother first!" He laughed again, thinking how surprised his grandmother would be if he should decide to sell her. Then he laughed still harder, until water began to slosh out of his cans. "If you want to buy a burro, I think Chucho would sell you that gray one of his for ten pesos, he is so mad at him."

"Where did you see Chucho?" asked Uncle Silván, trying not to seem excited.

"Down in front of the gate to the bull ring, pushing that stubborn animal of his along an inch at a time, with only half a load of wood on his back, too. I don't understand it. I have seen that burro happily carry a load five times as big." The small man went on with his heavy load of water, laughing at his own burro who looked like a pink haystack walking along on four slim legs.

Pablo knew why Angelito was being stubborn. He was lonesome.

"Ten pesos! Did you hear that?" chuckled Uncle Silván.

They found Chucho in front of the gate to the bull ring. He was picking up sticks of wood off the street and piling them on top of the loads of wood on the backs of his three brown burros. Angelito was not in sight anywhere. Chucho's face was so dark and angry that Uncle Silván decided to wait behind while Pablo went up and spoke to him.

"Did you sell Angelito?" asked the boy.

"Yes, I did!" said Chucho, banging another stick of wood on one of the loads so hard that it made the burro groan. "A few moments ago, I sold him for ten pesos, and he wasn't worth even that! Ever since that Uncle Silván of yours stole him from me, that animal has been impossible! Stopping stubbornly every three steps! Looking at me as if he wanted to eat me! He used to be like any other decent burro, never looking at anything." Chucho

was almost crying. "When you see that Uncle Silván of yours, you can tell him for me—" He noticed the old man slipping around a corner, but he was too tired from being angry to run after him. "You can tell that Uncle Silván of yours I have him to thank for spoiling my best burro." Chucho spoke to his three brown burros and followed them down the street.

Pablo wished he had thought to ask Chucho who had bought Angelito.

Star Stories

All afternoon, the boy wandered all over the quiet, lonely, sunny town, looking for Angelito, or for Uncle Silván. He could not find either of them.

Siesta ended with a booming of bells, and suddenly there were people everywhere, doing the same things they did every day at this time of the afternoon. Pablo was more lonely than ever.

And then, far away, over the cries of the people selling things, over the chirping of birds in the monkey trees, he heard a new sound—a sound of mariachi music, of guitars and singing. And he was sure that one voice, singing higher and louder and sadder than any of the others, was Uncle Silván's voice!

Pablo followed the threads of music and found where it was coming from. In a small cantina called "The Higher Emotions," in the dim light inside, there sat Uncle Silván, playing a shining new guitar and singing so high and loud that sometimes his mouth opened as wide as a frog's and the muscles in his neck seemed to twang like the strings on his guitar. He was wearing a fine new straw sombrero with spangles on it, and so were the other five men who were playing different sizes of guitars and singing with him. The song went on for a long time. At last it ended.

Uncle Silván slapped his guitar proudly and set it aside. He called to a man who brought in a tray covered with steaming *tamales* and glasses of pulque. All the mariachis began to eat and drink and tell Uncle Silván that he was their best friend. They thanked him over and over for the fine sombreros he had bought for them, and for the food, and told him the guitar he had bought in a pawn shop had the best tone in the world.

Peeking through the swinging doors, Pablo could see that Uncle Silván was having the best time he had ever had in his whole life. But it was pretty clear that he had forgotten about buying Angelito and had forgotten that the money he was spending was not his. It would not be his until he had worked in Miss Iris's garden for a whole month. And Pablo knew that Uncle Silván would never go back to that garden again.

He let the doors to the cantina swing shut. He went back to the town gardens and sat there until the sun went down and the moon came up. It was his fault that Miss Iris had paid Uncle Silván all that money. The only thing Pablo could do was to do the work himself.

Then he remembered his father, working alone in his fields, and he felt that he had to go home, this very night!

He went up the steep narrow street past the tanks and the bridge and the rushing stream until he came to the field of sunflowers. He found his serape still neatly folded under a flat stone. He put it over his shoulder and walked on through the moonlight, up to the top of the hill. There the road split into two roads, and he did not know which

one to take. He wrapped himself in his serape and lay down on the bare ground and watched the moon and the stars.

For a long way out from the moon, there were no stars. The wide silvery light seemed to melt them away. Toward the west, where the sky turned darker and darker blue, stars began to show again. They hung there bright and still in old designs that told stories not even books remembered. Only old men like his grandfather Pico, who was dead now, remembered them. This father of his father used to read the star stories, and Pablo remembered them. This quiet old man, who had never learned how to read books, must have been the brother of Don Francisco, who had read all the books in the world. It was strange how people became so different when they learned how to read books. Pablo knew that books were good, but only if you never forgot how to read the quiet stories in the stars. When you forgot this quietness, you became sad, like Don Francisco.

Pablo was sad now, because of the way Uncle Silván had behaved, and because he could not think how to tell Miss Iris what had happened, and because he had left his father to do all the work in his field alone. But as he lay there on the earth, wrapped up in his serape, reading the old stories in the stars, he felt as quiet inside as the night was all around him.

Pablo's serape was black, with four narrow red lines across it close to each end. It was tightly woven and light to carry, but still no storms could pound the cold and wet through it. He remembered when his mother had squashed some cactus insects and boiled them together with white wool. After a while, the wool came out dyed bright red. He remembered when she had spun the black and red wool into fine tight threads, and when his father had woven them, pounding each cross-thread down hard. Pablo's serape was made to last until he was grown up and could weave one for himself and give this smaller one to his own son. Felipe had woven it three summers ago, just before the coldest winter when they had to eat both sheep, the white one and then the black one. The boy loved this serape his father had woven for him. It was beautiful and warm and, like the stars, it seemed to tell an old and quiet story. Thinking about this story, he fell asleep.

Thursday Morning

When Pablo opened his eyes, the sun was beginning to peek over the rim of the earth, a small bright spot burning a bigger and bigger hole in the edge of a mountain. Then it broke free, blazing in the sky, and shadows were dusted over with a sunny haze.

It was a bright morning, but cold.

The boy stayed snug in his serape, smelling the smoke of burning wood that drifted up from the town. He could not see the town, or a single house or tree anywhere, or even a stone wall. The place where he had slept was on top of a wide bare hill.

He stood up and soaked in a little of the sun's warmth. Soon he was pleasantly warm. He folded his serape and hung it over his shoulder. He walked along the road to where it became two roads. One curved down into the valley. The other wound on over the low hills toward the mountains. That was the road, he was sure, that finally passed close to his home.

He began to imagine what was happening out there, so far away. Josefina had had her breakfast, and his father and mother were having theirs. The hen would be hungry again. She was scratching in the dust and talking about

81

what she had found. The goat had been milked by now; she had supped up a drink at the spring and was browsing away through the cactus. Doves were singing in the pepper tree.

Pablo knew it would be night before he got there. But the next morning, he would go out to the field with his father to help him dig up the old corn roots and burn them.

He turned back toward the town and listened. There was something strange about the town. He had not heard one bell ringing, or a rooster crowing, or a dog barking, or the shouting of children on their way to school. He almost wondered if there *was* a town over there. He walked back toward the sunflowers and the edge of the hill. Yes, there was the tower—and houses with smoke coming up from their chimneys and trees still in a cup of shadow. The only sound was a fly buzzing by. That was the only sound. It was very strange.

What Pablo did not know was that every Thursday nothing happened in San Miguel. It was not like Sunday, which was market day, when everyone came to town, when all the bells rang all morning, when everyone was noisily buying something or selling something or going to church. It was not like siesta time when there were always a few people wandering about, a few children playing tops or marbles, always a little noise from somewhere. On Thursdays, a tremendous stillness settled over the town. Nobody did anything at all except stand against sunny walls in the morning or sit in shady doorways in the afternoon, thinking only about the pleasure of doing nothing. But Pablo did not know this, and the stillness worried him.

82

He began to think about Miss Iris.

Suddenly he knew that he had to do the work she had paid Uncle Silván to do! He knew that if he did not, he could never come back in the spring to work for her and go to school. He was afraid of the strange stillness that hung over the town, but he went down the hill because he knew that he had to.

Promises

Miss Iris sat in a bright corner of her garden, soaking in the warmth of the morning sun. She was drinking a cup of tea while the maid cooked her breakfast. She was thinking about Pablo. She hoped he had found the burro he wanted and was now on his way back home. She knew that he would come back in the spring and work for her and go to school. She knew that what he promised to do he would do.

But Pablo's Uncle Silván was different. She did not ever expect to see that old man again. The only reason she had given him the money was to help Pablo.

Someone knocked at her gate, and she called, "Come in."

The gate opened. It was Pablo.

He walked up to her and stood looking at the ground.

She could tell that something was troubling him and guessed what it was. "Did your Uncle Silván run off with the money I gave him?"

Pablo nodded.

"Before you found Angelito?"

Again he nodded.

He looked at the flowers trying to grow against her patio wall and at the fat green weeds growing happily in the path and between the bricks of her terrace.

"Will you have breakfast with me, Pablo?" asked Miss Iris.

He sat on a chair beside the table. They both sat there, silent in the morning sunshine, silent even while the maid served their breakfast.

While he was eating, Pablo kept looking at her garden. When he had finished eating, he said, "I think there is *caliche* under your flowers."

"Caliche? Is that bad?"

"My father would say so. This morning I saw lots of it on the top of the hill. Nothing grows up there, not even weeds. Water cannot soak into caliche."

Miss Iris looked at the weeds growing happily between the bricks of her terrace. "Perhaps here is where the flowers should be," she said, "and the terrace should be over there against the wall."

"I think so," said Pablo.

She handed him a spoon. "Dig down around the flowers and see what you find."

He dug a little hole in the flower bed and pulled up a chunk of crumbly white rock. "This is caliche," he said. "It is not good for flowers."

"It would be a big job to change everything around."

"I can do it," said the boy. "I will need only a shovel."

"The tool house is out back," said Miss Iris.

He went out to get the shovel.

She smiled. A garden wasn't really very important to her, but Pablo was.

There was another knock at the gate, and she called out, "Come in."

The gate opened. A narrow face with dark eyes looked in. It was Don Francisco.

Miss Iris was surprised. Never before, as far as she knew, had the old gentleman ever gone outside his own garden, unless he had a formal invitation to a dinner party where all the guests were famous people. But there he was, early in the morning, at Miss Iris's gate, and he was smiling. Don Francisco was actually smiling!

"I have come to ask you," he said, "if you know where I might find my grandnephew, Pablo Pico."

Miss Iris knew that something good had happened to Don Francisco. There was only a little sadness in his eyes, and it wasn't the kind that he wrote into poems. It was just a little worry that he wasn't quite as important a person as he used to think he was. He smiled again and asked her to come and look at something outside the gate.

She glanced out through the gate and saw Don Francisco's servant Ernesto standing there, looking ashamed of himself as he always did. Miss Iris did not like Ernesto. He was tall and fat in the middle but had thin legs. His pants were always pulled up too far above his shiny black shoes. He walked like a cat trying to sneak up on something, and there was something in his small eyes that he was afraid someone would see.

Miss Iris went out through the gate. She knew there must be something else that Don Francisco wanted to show her. There was. Standing patiently in the street, not looking at anything, was a small gray burro.

"Is that Angelito?" she asked.

"I don't know his name." Don Francisco smiled. "But he is the finest burro in San Miguel."

The gate squeaked, and Pablo came out on the sidewalk. He stood looking at the burro, who lifted his head and looked at Pablo. Quietly the boy went over and put his arms around Angelito's neck, and Angelito wiggled his soft gray muzzle.

"I would like to make you a present of that burro, Pablo," said Don Francisco.

"How did you find him, señor?" asked the boy.

The old gentleman smiled proudly. "I sent Ernesto out to buy the finest burro in San Miguel. And he did—for three hundred pesos."

A sudden loud and angry shout made Don Francisco jump. Uncle Silván, who had come bouncing up on his bare feet, had shouted, "Three hundred pesos! That is not true!"

Don Francisco's dark eyes flashed. "Do you, Silván Ruiz, dare to say that I, Francisco Pico, am not telling the truth?"

"If you had any intelligence," Uncle Silván shouted, "you would see what an old fool you are!"

Don Francisco began to laugh, and Uncle Silván shouted louder than ever, "How could you know what the truth is, sitting forever up there in your garden, scribbling in a book!"

Suddenly Don Francisco was not angry any more. "You are right, Silván. All my life I have been trying to find out what the truth is, and all the time I have been looking in the wrong direction."

Uncle Silván was so surprised to have Don Francisco agree with him that all he could do was open and shut his mouth and wave his hands helplessly at nothing. He turned away and said, "Angelito is the burro I promised to buy for Pablo. I would like to keep my promise. I have the money right here to pay for him." He took off his new sombrero, and from under the band inside he took out a neatly folded ten-peso bank note.

"Ten pesos!" said Don Francisco in disgust.

"That is all I have," said Uncle Silván with a sigh.

"Never!" said Don Francisco.

Uncle Silván took in a deep breath and turned away.

"Never," said Don Francisco again, but not quite so stubbornly.

"I wish you would sell Angelito to Uncle Silván," said Pablo, "because he promised to buy him for me, and I do not like to feel ashamed of people who do not keep their promises, or people who are stubborn."

Don Francisco did not want Pablo to feel ashamed of him, and so he said, "All right. I will sell Angelito to Silván." Then he looked more stubborn than ever. "I will sell that burro for exactly what I paid for him!"

"This is what I will pay you." Uncle Silván smiled and held out the ten-peso note.

Don Francisco turned to Pablo and said a little stiffly, "First, you must promise me something."

"What, señor?" asked the boy.

"You must promise me that you will come to live in my house and let me send you to school."

Pablo looked carefully at Don Francisco Pico. He saw

how lonely the old man was—and that he really did like children. And Pablo understood something else about Don Francisco. Now that the hole in his wall was closed up and there was no way for children to peek in at him and talk to him, he was afraid of being lonelier than ever. He had complained for ten years about the hole's being there, so now he would be ashamed to have it opened up again. Pablo understood what the old man was thinking. "You would have to promise to stop being sad," he said.

"I promise," said Don Francisco, and he smiled hopefully to prove it.

"Then I will come back in the spring, after I have helped my father plant our corn."

The old gentleman sighed. "That is a long time to be lonely." He looked at Uncle Silván. It was hard for him to say, but he said it. "I will sell you the burro."

Uncle Silván gave him the ten pesos and said, very dignified, "I think you will find the rest of your three hundred pesos in Ernesto's pocket."

Ernesto knew that it would be no use trying to deceive Don Francisco. Sadly he pulled a crumpled bundle of money out of his pocket and handed it to Don Francisco.

"You should be ashamed!" said Uncle Silván to Ernesto. Then he turned to Miss Iris and asked, "How many days is one month divided by six?"

"Five days," she said.

Uncle Silván looked very sly. "So if six men worked for five days in your garden, that would be the same as one man working for one month. Yes?"

90

Miss Iris did not know what the old man was up to, but she was amused. "Yes," she said.

Uncle Silván went bouncing happily out into the street, waving his arms and shouting, and round the corner bounced his five mariachi friends, each wearing a beautiful new straw sombrero with spangles. The first one carried a pick, the second one carried a shovel, the third one carried a spade, the fourth one carried a paper sack full of something, and the fifth one carried by his yellow legs a big live rooster dangling upside down and looking around at everything with great curiosity.

Pablo's Return

By sunset, the rooster discovered that it was more comfortable to ride standing on Angelito's back than hanging upside down, dangling by his legs. Now he stood, proud in his beautiful feathers, riding in front of Pablo, bobbing his head, looking with great curiosity at the road, the faraway mountains, and the flaming clouds above the mountains.

When night fell, they rode on hour after hour through the stillness, until the moon went down behind the mountains. Then they slept, Angelito where he stood, Pablo on the ground wrapped up in his serape, and the rooster sitting on Angelito's back.

Suddenly the most terrific noise wakened Pablo!

The burro and the rooster had both noticed the first pale light of dawn in the sky, and both of them were shouting that it was already another day, or soon would be—another fine bright day. "Haw-hee-haw!" brayed Angelito, while the rooster on his back crowed, "Cock-a-doodle-doo!"

At first it was quite cold, but by the time Pablo rode down the hillside through the maguey plants, the sun was high and warm.

Felipe had noticed the shining cloud of pink dust a long way away. He was waiting for Pablo outside the cactus fence. But he hardly looked at the boy when he saw the rooster standing there on the burro, proudly ruffling his feathers and talking importantly about himself.

Angelito stood patiently while Pablo went over to his father and kissed his hand and gave him the paper sack full of presents from Uncle Silván.

Felipe could not take his eyes away from the rooster. "That is a fine rooster," he said.

The dusty hen seemed to think so, too, although she pretended not to notice him at all. She went on scratching in the dust and looking carefully where she had scratched, complaining because no matter how hard she scratched, she could not find anything worth eating.

The rooster suggested that he might be able to help her. He jumped down and told her that he would be glad to show her how to scratch. He made a very important business of scratching first with one yellow leg and then the other, and stepping back and looking closely at the ground, first with one eye and then the other. He told her to step over closer and he would show her what he had found— something tremendously important. She came over and looked at what he had scratched up. It was only a common small black beetle, nothing she would ever bother to eat. But she ate it anyway.

Felipe thought that he had never seen a more beautiful and gentlemanly rooster.

"He is a present to you from Uncle Silván," said Pablo.

"I did not know Silván was such a rich man, to be able to give that burro to you and a rooster to me."

"He bought those sandals for you, too. And ribbons for my mother."

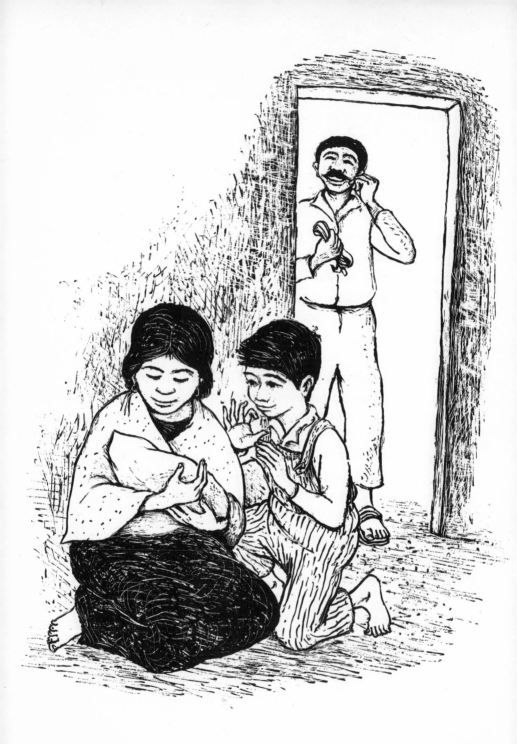

Felipe took the sandals out of the paper sack and sat down and put them on. They were as good as any he could have made himself. They must have cost a great deal. "Did you sell the corn?" he asked.

Pablo did not know how to tell what had happened to the corn. "Uncle Silván needed that corn very badly," he said.

Felipe was glad that it had been useful to Uncle Silván.

"Did you learn how to read?" Felipe asked. "But no, it takes a long time to learn how to read. Yes?"

"A long time," said Pablo. "I am going back to the town in spring, after our corn is planted. I am going to stay with your father's brother, Don Francisco Pico, and go to school, perhaps for many years."

"Don Francisco? My father had many brothers. I do not think I know that one." Felipe walked toward the house in his stiff new sandals. "Perhaps you would like to see *your* new brother who was born last night."

This was a wonderful surprise to Pablo. He went into the house and knelt beside his mother and kissed her hand. She held her new little baby up for him to see.

"What is his name?" asked Pablo softly.

"We have not yet found a name for him," said Maria.

Felipe gave her the ribbons Uncle Silván had sent to her. They were sky blue, like the niche where the sweet kind lady stands dreaming of all the wonderful things there are in heaven.

Maria thought there were a great many wonderful things on the earth, too. She listened to Josefina's baby laughter when Pablo hugged her and kissed her. She listened to the rooster talking importantly outside in the sunshine and to the doves singing in the pepper tree. The stillness of the world was full of pleasant sounds. She was very happy.

Felipe was standing where she could see the new sandals Uncle Silván had sent him. She thought they were very fine.

"Perhaps we might call our new baby Silván," said Pablo.

"It is a good name," said Felipe.

"Yes," said Maria. "Silván Pico. It is a good name."

With small careful steps, Angelito walked up to the door and looked in—at the new baby, at Maria and Josefina, at Felipe and Pablo. He had taken a drink at the spring and was now thoughtfully chewing a mouthful of weeds. He wiggled his soft gray muzzle to let them all know how happy he was to be their burro.

No one said anything about the letter Uncle Silván had brought to Maria. No one even thought about it. Whatever was in the letter, good or bad, it was not important.